To _Theo_

From _mAHA_

On _Christmas 2023_

Geor

The GRUMPY OLD OX

Anthony DeStefano

Illustrated by
Richard Cowdrey
New York Times Bestselling Artist

SOPHIA
INSTITUTE PRESS

Text Copyright © 2020 by Anthony DeStefano
Images Copyright © 2020 by Richard Cowdrey

Printed in the United States of America.

Sophia Institute Press®
Box 5284, Manchester, NH 03108
1-800-888-9344

www.SophiaInstitute.com
Sophia Institute Press® is a registered trademark of Sophia Institute.

Library of Congress Control Number:
9781644131787

Fifth Printing

This book is dedicated to my godson,
Michael Carmine Fagundes.

– Anthony DeStefano

To Mike Palumbo, who takes the
joy of Jesus wherever he goes.

– Richard Cowdrey

There once was an ox,
grumpy and old,
blind as a bat,
selfish and cold.

Prideful and lame,
with tired old bones,
he lived in a stable,
depressed and alone.

Without any family
and no friends in sight,
he stayed by himself
from morning till night.

His master, like him,
was stubborn and vain.
He owned a small inn
where visitors came.

He gave the ox orders;
the ox disobeyed.
Defiant and willful,
he wasn't afraid.

The man took a broom
and with a loud smack,
he gave the old ox
a whack on his back.

"You lazy and sightless
and smelly old brute,"
the innkeeper shouted
and kicked with
his boot.

The ox simply sneered
and grumbled with pride.
He limped to the stable
and lay down inside.

The stable was dark,
but he didn't mind.
He stayed there alone,
just bitter and blind.

Then one black night
the door opened wide.
A man and a woman
were standing outside.

The owner was with them;
he said with a grin:
"You'll have to stay here—
no room at my inn!"

The ox strained his eyes,
attempting to see.
He barely detected
the forms of all three.

The lady was pregnant
and heavy with child.
The man held her hand
and tenderly smiled.

He put a small blanket
on top of the dirt.
The woman lay down,
about to give birth.

The innkeeper left them
all cold and alone,
without any food
and so far from home.

But something odd happened
that memorable night—
something that gave
the ox quite a fright.

A shutter flew open
and in flooded light.
A star in the heavens
was dazzlingly bright.

It made the small stable
feel pleasant and warm.
In this simple setting
the child was born.

Strange as it seems,
the ox became sad
because the young family
was treated so bad.

"I'm all by myself,"
the grumpy ox sighed.
"The reason is that
I'm so full of pride.
But this little babe,
so humble and poor,
is guiltless and precious
and perfect and pure."

Just at that moment
he had an idea.
He struggled to stand
and limped over near
the manger he ate from
(all filled up with straw),
and pulled it across
the cold stable floor.

He looked at the woman;
in ox-talk he said:
"Take my straw manger
for your baby's bed."

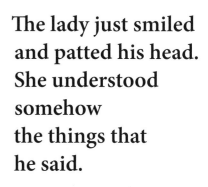

He limped to the pail
from which he drank water.
He picked up the handle
and carried it toward her.

He put the pail down
and said with a bow:
"Wash him with this.
I'm not thirsty right now."

The lady just smiled
and patted his head.
She understood
somehow
the things that
he said.

She bathed her small baby
and dressed him in white.
He slept in the manger
throughout the cold night.

Soon shepherds came in
along with their sheep.
They knelt by the crib
and watched the babe sleep.

A donkey and camel
came through the door.
They walked very slowly
and knelt on the floor.

Three figures followed:
each wore a crown,
each bearing gifts,
each kneeling down.

"What can be happening?
Who can this be?"
The grumpy ox squinted.
"I wish I could see!"

He strained with his eyes
and thought for a while;
then looked at the child
and started to smile.

"This baby is special,
sent down from above.
Yes, that's why this stable
is so filled with love.
That's why these people
are worshipping him.
He must be from God.
He must be a king!"

The rest of the night
he knelt on the earth,
next to the feet
of the girl who gave birth.

The family soon left
to find a new home.
With everyone gone
the ox was alone.

He thought of the babe,
so loved and adored,
while he, the old ox,
was shunned and ignored.

"I'll try to be different,"
the grumpy ox swore.
"I won't be so prideful
or mean anymore!"

He walked to the manger;
his hunger was great.
He stuck his head in
and rapidly ate.

Then he felt thirsty
and looked over where
the babe had been bathed
in the bucket with care.

He drank from the pail
until he was done
and soon fell asleep
outside in the sun.

He slept and he slept
and he slept through the night.
He rose with the dawn
In the soft golden light.

But when he awoke
and opened his eyes,
the ox was amazed
by a wondrous surprise.

He looked all around
and what did he find?
He couldn't believe—
he no longer was blind!

The hillside, the village,
the stable, the tree—
all that he gazed at
was plain as could be!

He rubbed both his eyes,
then rubbed them again.
Now he saw donkeys
and camels and men.

All that was blurry
was now crystal clear.
Even the mountains
appeared very near.

He got to his feet
and walked through the field.
His leg was all better;
his limp had been healed!

He ran to the stable
and danced through the door.
He didn't feel grumpy
or old anymore.

The ox was so grateful
he started to sing.
"It must be a gift,
a gift from the king—
the baby from Heaven,
it just has to be.
I drank of the water
and now I feel free!
I ate from the manger
and now I can see!"

He started to cry
and shouted with glee:
"I can see, I can see;
at last I can see!"

From the Bible

She wrapped [the baby] in swaddling clothes
and laid him in a manger, because there was
no room for them in the inn.

– LUKE 2:7 (NABRE)

The ox knows its master, the donkey its
owner's manger, but…my people do not
understand.

– ISAIAH 1:3 (NIV)

The Spirit of the Lord is upon me,
because he has anointed me
to bring glad tidings to the poor.
He has sent me to proclaim liberty to captives
and recovery of sight to the blind…

– LUKE 4:18 (NABRE)

THE MAN
WHO COULD
CALL DOWN OWLS

EVE BUNTING

THE MAN
WHO COULD
CALL DOWN OWLS

ILLUSTRATED BY

CHARLES MIKOLAYCAK

MACMILLAN PUBLISHING COMPANY
NEW YORK

COLLIER MACMILLAN PUBLISHERS
LONDON

Macmillan Publishing Company
866 Third Avenue, New York, N.Y. 10022
Collier Macmillan Canada, Inc.

Printed in the United States of America

10 9 8 7 6 5 4 3 2

Library of Congress Cataloging in Publication Data

Bunting, Eve, date.
The man who could call down owls.
Summary: When a stranger takes away the powers of an
old man who has befriended owls, the vengeance wreaked
on him is swift and fitting.
[1. Owls—Fiction] I. Mikolaycak, Charles, ill.
II. Title.
PZ7.B91527Man 1984   [E]   83-17568
ISBN 0-02-715380-0

*For Candy Dean, who told me
about the man who could call down owls*

—E.B.

To Sido Farina

—C.M.

There was once a man who could call down owls. He wore a cloak of softest white and a wide hat with a feather in it, and he carried a willow wand.

Every night, when the dark came, the owl man walked into the woods and stopped at the first clearing. Every night, a scattering of people from the village followed to watch. The boy Con, who lived in the village too, always came.

The owl man stared into the trees. He had shadows on his face but not in his eyes and he made no sound.

The watchers, too, stayed quiet and at a distance.

The owl man stretched his willow wand to the night sky.

And the owls came.
They came swooping on noiseless wings.
To perch on his shoulders.
To perch on his wand.
To gather on branches closest to where he stood.
Always, the owls came.

By day the man worked in his owl barn. There were wings to be mended and legs to be splinted.

"How do you find the owls that need your help?" the boy asked.

The man smiled. "They find me." He held a screech owl. "When an owl is sick and frightened you must hold it firmly. Then it can't hurt itself or you. Always remember that."

"I will remember," Con said. "But I wish I knew the owls as you do."

"You will learn."

And now, in the night clearing, the boy moved to the man's side, quietly as an owl in flight.

"What kind is that?" he whispered.

"Barn owl." The man's voice was high and for a minute Con thought the sound of it was the sound of wind in the trees.

The barn owl swiveled its white, flower face, raised its wings, then closed itself again.

An owl no bigger than a sparrow came to nestle in the shadow of the wide hat.

"Elf owl." The man smoothed the pale chest feathers till the owl eyes closed.

Deep in the dark of the trees was a hoot, hoot, hooting and a great horned cut the air to land on a stunted branch, so close that the boy could see the ring of white feathers that lay mysteriously at its throat.

Owls everywhere. And the man in the middle, his cloak drifting about him like marsh mist, and Con, always Con, and the man with the owls around him.

One night a stranger came. His eyes narrowed when the owls dropped from the trees. He stepped close.

"A man who can command the birds of the air has power indeed!" he whispered.

"He does not command," Con said. But the stranger was not listening.

At the next dusk, the man who could call down owls did not walk on the path that led to the woods. The stranger walked. He wore the white cloak and the broad-brimmed hat and in his hand was the willow wand.

Con ran to tug at his cloak. "Where is the man who can call down owls? What have you done with him?"

The stranger pushed the boy aside.

"You took his cloak and his hat and his willow wand," Con said.

"He gave them to me."

"He would never give them."

The stranger smiled. "I took them, then, and his power along with them."

The stranger's smile was cold as death and Con was afraid.

The people clustered behind as the stranger entered the clearing. And it was then that Con saw the great snowy owl. He caught his breath. Never had he seen such a rare and beautiful owl. It shimmered above the clearing, its giant wings whitening the earth below. And Con knew how the stranger came by the cloak and the hat and the willow wand. And he knew that the owl was the man and the man the owl, and that the man who could call down owls would never return.

The stranger raised the wand to point to the moon.

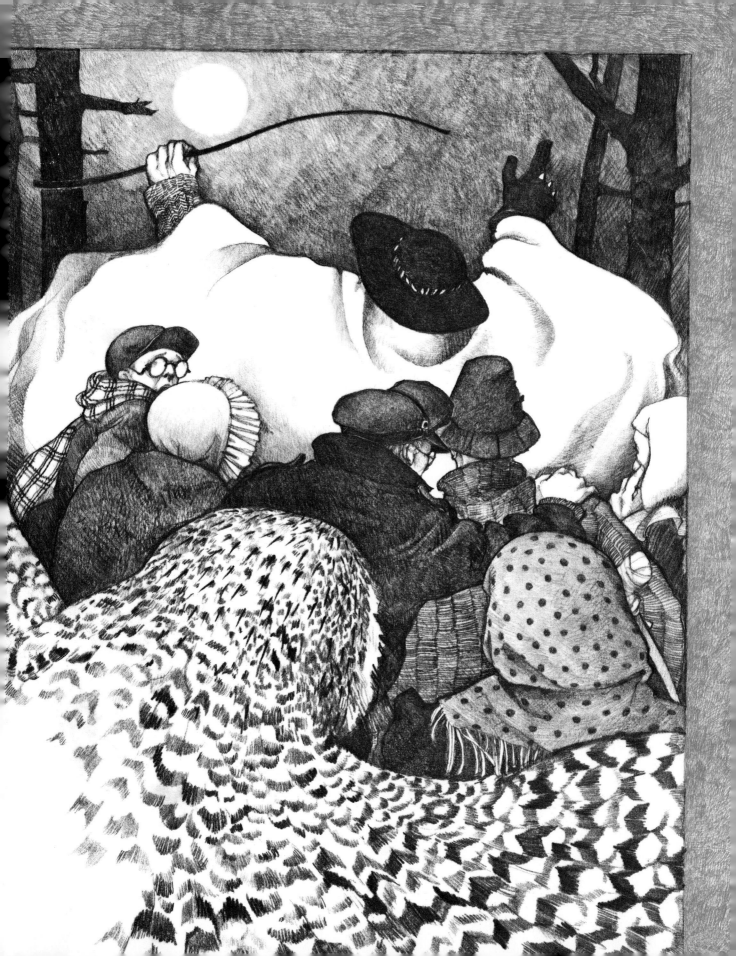

And the owls came.

Con had never seen so many. The sky moved with them.

A hawk owl dropped on pointed wings to hover over the stranger's head, then dived, its talons raking the hat and the hands that the stranger raised to protect himself.

A great gray came, its flight slow and measured. It came silently, on straightened legs, and its beak found the stranger's cheek, and there were other owls, swooping, shearing, searing. The air hissed to the beat

of wings and the stranger was crawling for the shelter
of the trees, running now, the white cloak falling from
him to lie in a drift of snow.

He was gone, and so were the owls. And the people stood, mute, frightened.

Above, the great snowy melted upward to fade into the clouds that covered the moon, drifted up and was gone too.

Then the owls came, swooping on noiseless wings.

To perch on the boy's shoulders.

To perch on his head.

To gather on branches closest to where he stood.

Chirping and screeching and filling the night with love, the owls came.

This book was set in 14-point Trump.
The text was composed by Cardinal Typographers.
Printing and binding were done by
Halliday Lithograph, an Arcata Company.

Typography and binding design by
Charles Mikolaycak and Ellen Weiss.

The drawings were rendered actual size
in pencil on a natural vellum paper
manufactured by Canson & Montgolier Mills
in France.